WALT DISNEY'S
ALICE in WONDERLAND

Adapted by Teddy Slater
Illustrated by Franc Mateu

A GOLDEN BOOK • NEW YORK
Western Publishing Company, Inc., Racine, Wisconsin 53404

One golden spring day a young girl named Alice was sitting by the river, listening to her sister read aloud from a history book. At least, that's what Alice was supposed to be doing. Instead, she was playing with Dinah, her cat, which was more fun.

"I wish you could talk back to me, Dinah," she said.
"I'm sure you would have many interesting things to say."
    The sun was so bright, and the air was so warm, that
Alice was soon daydreaming. Slowly her head began
to nod.

She snapped to attention, however, when a large
white rabbit went dashing by. Strangely, he was
wearing a waistcoat and a bow tie and carrying a huge
pocket watch. Even more strangely, he was talking to
himself!

"I'm late, I'm late, for a very important date," the
White Rabbit muttered as he went along.

In a flash Alice was on her feet, chasing after him.

Still fretting, the rabbit took a giant hop into a hollow tree, exclaiming, "Oh, my fur and whiskers! I'm late, I'm late, I'm late!"

Alice thought that he might be late for a party, so she followed him into the tree. Suddenly she stumbled, then tumbled head over heels into a deep hole. After a while, instead of falling faster and faster, she began to fall slower and slower—until she was floating more than falling.

Alice landed gently, just in time to see the rabbit's white puff of a tail disappear behind a tiny door.

Alice was too big to follow him, but she soon
discovered that she had entered a strange and
wondrous land. It was full of the oddest creatures she
had ever seen. There were talking birds and walking
fish. There was also a Cheshire cat, with the widest of

grins, who kept appearing and disappearing. And sometimes only the cat's grin could be seen.

Alice thought the creatures all seemed quite at home in this topsy-turvy Wonderland. She hoped one of them could help her find the White Rabbit, but they were no help at all.

Alice walked through a forest and came across a pair of roly-poly twins. Their names were written on their collars. "I see that you are Tweedledee and Tweedledum," she greeted them.

"When first meeting someone, you should shake hands and state your name and business," said Tweedledum, grabbing Alice's hand.

"That's manners!" said Tweedledee, grabbing her other hand.

With that, the tubby twins danced Alice around and swept her off her feet. But they were so rough that they flipped her over and knocked her onto her back. Alice was not amused.

Then Tweedledee and Tweedledum started to tell her a fanciful story that she couldn't understand. Despite the twins' protests, Alice continued on her way to search for the White Rabbit.

Soon she came to an unusual garden. There Alice
discovered that even the flowers of Wonderland could
speak!

"What kind of flower are you?" a big red rose asked
her.

"Oh, I'm not any kind of flower," Alice replied.

"No fragrance," a daisy said, sniffing at Alice's hair.

"But I'm not a flower," Alice repeated.

"Just as I suspected," the rose cried. "She's nothing but a common weed!"

"Leave!" shouted all the flowers together. "We don't want you in our lovely garden." Alice was forced to run away.

Near the garden Alice saw a familiar grin up in a tree. It was the Cheshire Cat. When the rest of him appeared, Alice said politely, "Have you seen the White Rabbit?"

"No," said the Cheshire Cat. "But if I were looking for him, I'd ask the Mad Hatter."

"Goodness," said Alice, "I'm not sure I want to visit a mad person."

"You can't avoid it," said the cat. "Mostly everyone here is mad." And with that, the cat began to disappear.

"Wait, please!" Alice cried. "You haven't told me where the Mad Hatter lives." But it was too late.

As Alice wandered on she saw two road signs pointing in the same direction. One read "Mad Hatter" and the other read "March Hare." Alice still had no wish to meet a Mad Hatter, but she hoped the March Hare might know the mysterious White Rabbit, too.

Alice followed the signs to a clearing in the woods,
where the Mad Hatter was giving a tea party.

"No room!" the Mad Hatter howled as Alice
plopped down in one of the many empty chairs around
the table.

"But there's plenty of room," Alice protested.

"Perhaps," the March Hare admitted. "But it's very rude to sit down without first being invited."

The Hatter and the Hare then proceeded to make Alice feel quite unwelcome. They not only refused to give her any tea, but it was clear that they had no intention of helping her find the White Rabbit. So once again, Alice set off on her own.

Alice soon came across one of the strangest creatures she would meet in this very strange land—the Queen of Hearts. Though the Queen was dressed like an ordinary queen in an ordinary deck of cards, her manner was most regal as she ordered her subjects around.

The Queen was playing croquet when Alice appeared. This being Wonderland, however, it was not like any croquet game Alice had ever seen. The wickets were made of cards, the balls were hedgehogs, and the mallets were bright pink flamingos.

The Queen politely invited her to play, and Alice thought she'd give it a try. It might, she thought, be fun. But it wasn't! Alice's flamingo didn't seem at all cooperative, and the Queen turned out to be a truly terrible sport. "Off with his head!" she cried the minute anyone displeased her.

Alice considered leaving the game. After all, she very much wanted to keep her head. But she also wanted to meet the White Rabbit. And she had a feeling he was very near indeed.

As it turned out, Alice did see the White Rabbit. He was working for the Queen. Alice was just about to introduce herself to him when the Cheshire Cat made another of his unannounced appearances.

Alice watched in horror as the mischievous cat tripped up the Queen and then promptly disappeared. And when the Queen turned accusing eyes on Alice, crying, "Off with her head!" Alice decided it was time for her, too, to disappear.

Without so much as a hello or a good-bye to the
White Rabbit, Alice took off into the woods. Faster
and faster she ran till she tripped headlong over a root
and once more found herself whirling and swirling
through time and space....

"Please wake up, Alice," she heard a soft voice say.

Alice awoke with a start, back on the riverbank.
Dinah the cat was curled up in her lap.

"You've been dreaming," said Alice's sister.

"Oh, dear," Alice cried. "I must have fallen asleep while you were reading to me."

"It's been a long day," said her sister. "No wonder you're tired. Why don't we just go home now and have our tea?"

"I seem to have lost my taste for tea," Alice said, recalling the Mad Hatter's tea party, "but I certainly would like to go home."

Alice's sister gave her a puzzled look. Then she took Alice's hand and they walked home together.